# When You've Got to Go!

by Mitchell Kriegman
illustrated by Kathryn Mitter

Simon Spotlight

New York     London     Toronto     Sydney     Singapore

Based on the TV series *Bear in the Big Blue House*™
created by Mitchell Kriegman. Produced by
The Jim Henson Company for Disney Channel.

SIMON SPOTLIGHT
An imprint of Simon & Schuster Children's Publishing Division
1230 Avenue of the Americas
New York, New York 10020
Manufactured in the United States of America
First Edition     10 9 8 7 6 5 4 3 2 1
ISBN: 0-689-83380-6

One morning at the Big Blue House, Bear and Tutter were playing a friendly game of checkers.

"So, Tutter, have you figured out your next move?" Bear asked.

"I don't know, Bear. I don't know," Tutter said, squirming. "Sometimes it's just so hard to think!"

Bear was worried. He could tell that Tutter had to go to the bathroom.
"Tutter, if you have to go to the bathroom, it's okay," Bear said.

"But I don't want to, Bear! I'm winning! I'm winning!" Tutter
squeaked, dancing from side to side.

"You know, if you ever have to go to the bathroom, you should,
even if you're in the middle of doing something or having fun,"
Bear said.

"But what about our game?" Tutter asked.

"The game will still be here when you come back, and you'll still be winning," Bear told his friend. "I'll be glad to wait for you."

"Great, Bear," Tutter squeaked. "Because I really have to go!" Tutter jumped up from the table and rushed off to his mouse hole.

"Is everything all right in there, Tutter?"
Bear asked.

"Fine, Bear, fine! I just had to poop!" Tutter answered.

Bear was glad Tutter was taking care of himself. "Well, take your time. There's no hurry," Bear said.

"I know, Bear. I always take my time when I use the potty," Tutter said proudly. "Sometimes I even look at a picture book. But now I've got to wipe myself and wash my hands!"

Soon Tutter came out of his mouse hole humming a happy tune.
"Ahhh! I feel much better now, Bear. Much better!" he said.
"That's great . . . but are you sure you did everything?"
Bear asked.
"Well, I used the potty, then I wiped,
then I washed my hands, and then . . .
oh my!" Tutter exclaimed. He rushed
back into his mouse hole.
"Flushing is important, too!"
Bear said as he heard Tutter
flush the toilet.

Bear and Tutter went back to their game of checkers. Suddenly they heard Treelo calling.

"Come quick, Bear. Come quick! Ojo needs help!" Treelo cried.

"I'll be right back, Tutter," Bear said. He hurried up the stairs.

When Bear got upstairs, Treelo pointed to the bathroom. The door was closed.

"Ojo, are you okay in there?" Bear called.

"Yes, Bear. I just needed some privacy," Ojo said. "But I could use a little help, too."

Bear opened the door and found Ojo sitting on the potty.
"So, Ojo, what's going on?" Bear asked.
"Well, Treelo and I were playing hide-and-seek," Ojo explained.
"I knew I had to go to the bathroom, but I didn't get to
the potty in time!" She looked a little upset.

"That's okay, Ojo," Bear said. "Accidents can happen to anyone. It's great that you did your best to get to the potty."

"Really?" Ojo said. She felt much better. When she was done, she wiped, hopped off the potty, and flushed it.

As Ojo washed her hands, she asked Bear, "I was wondering . . . what should you do if you need to go to the bathroom and you're not at home?"

"Good question, Ojo!" Bear said. "You know, it's fine to ask 'May I use the bathroom?' or 'Where is the bathroom?' That way grown-ups will know you have to go to the potty and can show you where the bathroom is."

Ojo dried her hands on a towel. "Well, I've washed up!" she exclaimed. "I'm ready to play again. Thanks, Bear!"

Just as Ojo left, Treelo jumped into the bathroom.

"Ahhh! Treelo, you surprised me!" Bear said with a laugh.

"Where do the poop and pee go when you flush the toilet?" Treelo asked Bear.

"That's a good question," Bear said.

"When you flush the toilet, the poop and pee
go down the pipes and under the house and are washed away."

"Bye-bye!" Treelo said, waving at the toilet.

"Come on, Treelo," Bear said. "Let's find Tutter and finish that
game of checkers."

The game was soon finished, all right. Tutter was about to beat Bear!

"I won! I won!" Tutter exclaimed as he made the last move.

"Yes," Bear agreed. "You won! You're a very good checker player, Tutter."

Just then Ojo, Pip, and Pop came in. Ojo was very excited. "Bear, you've got to hear this!" she exclaimed. "It's about The Mystic Order of Toileteers."

"Toileteers? What are Toileteers?" Tutter asked.

"It's a special club for everyone who uses . . ." Pip began.

"Or is going to use . . ." Pop continued.

"The potty!" Pip and Pop said together.

"I want to join! I use the potty!" Tutter said, jumping up and down.

"Me too!" said Treelo.

"And me!" Ojo said.

"Well, Pip and Pop, tell us about it!" Bear said.

Pip and Pop told their friends all the great things about being a Toileteer, like wearing underwear instead of diapers and always feeling clean. Ojo, Tutter, and Treelo all wanted to join, so Pip and Pop made them members. Now everyone was a Toileteer!

Later that night, Bear told Luna about how everyone was learning to use the potty.

"That's wonderful," Luna said. "You know, I've always wanted to tell the little ones that even after they stop wearing diapers, they can still be kids. Their mommies and daddies will still take care of them."

"That's true, Luna," said Bear. "When you learn to use the potty and leave your diapers behind, you don't have to give up the other things you like, like hugs and cuddles."

"You're right, Bear," Luna agreed.

Bear said good night to Luna, and just before he turned out the light, he had one more thing to say:

"Remember, if you want to use the potty, all you have to do is listen to your body. You'll know when you've got to go!"